THE ARRANGEMENT

A REAL MAN

JENIKA SNOW

THE ARRANGEMENT (A REAL MAN)

By Jenika Snow

www.JenikaSnow.com

Jenika_Snow@Yahoo.com

Copyright © April 2020 by Jenika Snow

First ebook edition © April 2020 by Jenika Snow

Cover design by: Lori Jackson Design

Content Editor: Kayla Robichaux

Image provided by: Adobe Stock

THE ARRANGEMENT

Lenora

He hated me.

I loved him.

I had feelings for Beckham for so long it was a part of me now. But because his father married my mother, I knew there was no chance of us ever being together. We couldn't cross that line. I wouldn't for fear of ruining our relationship.

But then my mother betrayed his father, destroying our family and ripping Beckham from me.

Hurtful things were said, things that broke my heart.

I never thought I'd see him again. It was an unmeasurable pain.

And six months later, I found myself having to turn to him, the man I loved.... the man who hated me.

He agreed to let me stay with him until I was on my feet again. But what arrangement did he have in mind? What did he want as payment?

Beckham

She thought I hated her.

She couldn't be further from the truth.

I was so in love with her that no one else mattered. But I screwed that up in one moment of pain, in one second of hurt.

It wasn't even her fault, but I'd taken it out on Lenora. And I regretted it every day since. I wanted to call her so many times. I'd driven by her house like a stalker, wanting to talk to her, to beg for forgiveness.

But now was my time to make things right.

Now was my chance to prove to her I'd do whatever it took to have her forgive me... to have her love me too.

CHAPTER ONE

Lenora

I WONDERED if I was making the biggest damn mistake of my life. But desperation had people doing crazy shit, and moving in with my stepbrother, the one I'd wanted since the first day his father married my mother and he joined my family, was pretty high on the last of insane shit.

The cab pulled up in front of the house, and all I could do was sit there looking at the small two-story structure, wondering if I could have gone another route. I hadn't spoken to Beckham in almost six months—well, hadn't talked to him up until I called him last month and all but begged for his help.

Jobless, nearly penniless, and refusing to call my

mother for help, I knew he was the only other person I could rely on.

My life had gone down the shit drain, and there was nothing I could do to stop it.

Months ago, our parents divorced when it was revealed that mother had a longstanding affair with one of her students at the university. I'd never seen hatred from Beckham before, but that day... I'd seen pure rage from him reflected toward my mom, and me as well.

Like I had something to do with it.

But I supposed I might have felt the same way if the roles had been reversed, angry that our family unit had been broken up by infidelity, that a broken home was our story now.

So I got it, and that's why it had been so hard for me to call Beckham and ask for help, to see if I could stay with him until I got my shit in order.

Did he still project his anger at me because of what my mother had done, how she'd shown no remorse over her actions? A part of me hated her for that too, and that's why I'd barely spoken to her since... because she truly didn't think she'd done anything wrong.

"Miss?"

I glanced over at the driver. He was staring at me,

this expectant look on his face, the unspoken "can you get the fuck out of my car?" expression on his face pretty loud.

He was probably wondering what in the hell my problem was, why I was just sitting here staring at my destination and not getting out of his damn car.

I reached in my pocket and grabbed my money, giving him what I owed and climbing out. He popped the trunk, not even bothering to help me with my bag, and as soon as I grabbed it and closed the door, he was driving off, leaving me there to face this myself. I looked at the house again, my heart in my throat.

As I stood there for long moments just staring at Beckham's house, a part of me wanted to just turn around and start walking, to not look back, to not worry about what all this meant. I replayed the last thing he said to me on the phone when I had to beg —humiliate myself in asking for help.

"Oh, don't worry, Lenora. I'll think of some way for you to repay me."

His voice had been so deep and coaxing, and I pictured him smiling, a shit-eating grin playing across his too handsome face as he spoke those words. I didn't know what kind of payment he was referring to, but I knew it wouldn't be the monetary kind.

Beckham hated me, and I knew he'd make me pay in more than one way.

And that scared me most of all.

CHAPTER TWO

Beckham

I saw the cab pull to a stop at the curb, and I stood there, looking out the window, watching as Lenora stayed in the vehicle and stared at my house. Even from a distance, I could tell she was nervous, afraid.

And I didn't blame her.

We'd left on fucking awful terms six months ago, and that was all my fault. I'd been so angry and hurt, using that to fuel my emotions and projecting them onto her, because she'd been right there. God, I'd been a bastard that day, and it haunted me ever since.

But seeing my father's heart break because the love of his life—her mother—had been having an affair had been the hardest thing I'd ever witnessed. And I'd taken it out on Lenora.

And as soon as I said the hurtful things, as soon as that shit spewed from my mouth, I wished I could have taken it back. I'd wanted to go back in time and repair the damage I caused between us.

Every day, I wanted to call her up and apologize. The things I said had made tears well up in her eyes... things that made me feel as if I were nothing more than a piece of shit on the bottom of someone's shoe.

But my anger and the betrayal made me a prideful bastard. And I hadn't apologized, I hadn't said anything to her since then.

Six fucking months of me being a worthless fuck and too afraid to confront her had ruined my happiness and any hope I could repair the damage.

And every single day, I hated my fucking self even more because of it. So when she called me just last month, asking for my help, I knew I had to make things right. It had to be fate that had her coming into my life once more.

I had to show her I'd been wrong, that what happened wasn't her fault, that no matter what, no matter how things ended, she'd always have me in her life. I'd always have her back.

I watched as she finally started walking toward the house, her nervousness, her fear, clear on her face. I thought about her phone call, how she asked for a place to stay and that she'd pay me back. And I told her we'd find some way that she could.

I didn't even know why I said it, didn't know why I thought it would be a good idea to end the conversation on that note. She probably thought I was some dirty bastard, that I would be cruel to her. I didn't blame her for thinking that. It wasn't like I'd shown her anything different.

Because the truth was... I loved Lenora. I always had. Ever since my father married her mom and we moved in together. Ever since I saw how sweet and kind she was, how smart and beautiful she was.

Ever since I realized my life would never be the same without her in it.

And I'd fucked it up.

But now was my chance to make things right. We'd made the arrangement for her to live with me until she got on her feet. But what she didn't know, what she'd find out sooner rather than later, was that I wasn't going to let her leave. I would show her she was meant to be mine. Always.

I'd show her how wrong I'd been, that if I could take it back, I would.

I'd show her that even though I'd fucked up, I could make things right.

I'd fall to my hands and knees and beg for forgiveness.

But the wound it caused her was no doubt deep, and whether she believed me or not was another story.

CHAPTER THREE

Lenora

MY HEART WAS THUNDERING as I knocked on the front door and then took a step back, as if that foot of space would have some kind of shield, be some kind of wall to protect me. For six months, I replayed Beckham's words in my head over and over again, this broken record that dug into my heart. They not only hurt because I cared about him, because he'd been part of my family—my life—but also because of how I felt for him on a more romantic level.

Because I was in love with him.

To this day, I still remember the progression of my feelings for him, how at first I'd noticed how attractive he was, then got to know him and loved his personality. He put on a good show of acting like he had no worries or cares, almost this aloofness about him. He was charismatic, and although he'd been the new guy at school, everyone had flocked to him. He was important.

And he always put me first, always made me feel as if no one could touch me, that I was better than anything that was negative and thrown in my way.

And as the years passed and we grew from teenagers to young adults, I found myself falling for him—maybe an inappropriate reaction because of what we were to each other, but a reality nonetheless.

But his words and anger had touched me, broken me. They'd crumbled and ruined the love I hoped—imagined—having with him one day.

But here I was, destiny and circumstance throwing a wrench in the mix and threatening to open up the wound in my heart once more.

And when that front door opened, I felt like everything around me froze, time standing still. My heart was the only thing in motion, beating rapidly against my ribs, painful and loud. Would he be able to hear it? I felt beads of sweat along my temples and gripped my bag tighter. Inside were my basic necessities. Everything else I accumulated over the years was in the storage facility, one that had been prepaid. One that only had one more month left. After that, I'd lose everything.

But I hoped while staying with Beckham and saving up money that I'd been able to find another place. Then I'd be able to figure out what I was going to do with my life.

Until then, I'd stay out of his way, mind my business, and keep my head down.

He held the door open with one hand, his other one extended as he braced it on the door frame. He said nothing as he stared at me. And I couldn't read his expression, because he was stoic, silent.

I tipped my head back slightly to look into his face. Beckham was a big guy, tall with a muscular build. But he wasn't too bulky, not like a bodybuilder, but more powerful than a swimmer. And seeing him again after six months had me feeling like I'd fallen right back down that rabbit hole of emotions.

I'd pushed down how I felt for him from all the hurt and anger. It had been a survival tactic, I supposed. But now I felt it rising up violently to the surface. I swallowed it down, bit my tongue to stop from crying—that pain a wakeup call—and reminded myself why I was standing at his doorstep.

Because I was desperate.

I didn't miss how he eyed me up and down, his gaze raking over my body and making me feel bare. I didn't know what I expected, but the slow smile that crept across his face wasn't one of them. I supposed I expected him to be cold and have nothing but an attitude. But he said nothing as he stepped aside and pushed the door open even more, allowing me to enter. Maybe he could see the desperation on my face, the complete hopelessness I felt. I'd hit rock-bottom, and how sad was my life, how lonely and pathetic was I that the one person who hated me the most was the only person I could turn to?

Once I was inside with my back to him, I heard the door shut. I didn't even know if I could speak right now, but I did turn around, facing him. He wore a blank expression on his face, and I didn't know why that made me as nervous as it did.

After we parted ways so horribly, and after the hurt had settled, I felt anger, wanting to curse him out, ask how he could treat me like shit after all those years, after how close we'd been... or how close I thought we'd been. But I'd taken the high road, kept my mouth shut, kept my distance, and just let that hurt and anger fester inside me. That's all I could do.

"Thank you again for letting me stay here." I cleared my throat, my voice low, scratchy. I swallowed roughly and just stared at him as he watched me. "Believe me," I said when he had yet to respond. "I wouldn't have called you if I wasn't at absolute rock-bottom." I was humiliated admitting that to him.

I ran my free hand down my jeans, willing it not to shake.

"You're fine, Lenora. Everything will be fine."

I cleared my throat. I wanted to believe him.

"How is your mom?" There was no accusation in his voice, just genuine curiosity. Or maybe he was just trying to start a conversation. Although that was the last thing I wanted to talk about, and I'm sure it was the same for him.

I scoffed before I could stop myself. "The same," I said with disgust. "But I haven't really spoken to her since that all...." I stopped myself and cleared my throat. Although my mom did reach out every now and then, she was far too consumed with her own life to care about much else other than herself, even if that something else was her only daughter.

And as Beckham stared at me, I knew I shouldn't have said anything, shouldn't have even went on about it. There was this thickness hanging between us, this never-ending pressure. And as I stared into his amber-colored eyes, I found myself whispering, "You weren't the only one she hurt, Beckham."

After my mother's infidelity had come to light, the fact that she had a lack of remorse, even her arrogance over it, had shifted everyone's life for the worse. At least *I* felt this shift inside me for the worse where she was concerned. She'd never been a very present mother to begin with, throwing herself into work, away more time than she was present.

Hell, I hadn't even been a planned pregnancy, but instead a wrench thrown in her young life after she'd had a short fling with a wealthy, much older man. And the latter had been the only piece of information she'd ever given me about who my father was.

Self-absorbed—my mother's picture would be under the definition in the dictionary.

I suppose that's why she found herself in the situation she was, in a torrid affair with one of her university students, who she was currently still seeing and living with in another state. Her affair had been quite public, very messy, yet she refused to apologize, to even acknowledge that she'd done anything wrong.

And her moving away hadn't just been about her

wanting to have this whirlwind romance with her new beau. It had been a scandal. She'd lost her position at the university, and she'd been humiliated.

She'd never admit it, but she's the one who lost the most.

But the truth was—and it was depressing to admit this about my own mother—but her being gone was a blessing in disguise. It gave me freedom. It let me breathe for once in my life.

Even if said life was currently up shit creek and I didn't have a paddle.

Beckham gave a short nod, and I pulled myself back to the present. I saw his expression soften a bit, but neither of us spoke. Maybe he saw the look on my face, knew where my thoughts had gone.

He finally cleared his throat and lifted his hand to rub the back of his neck. "Let me show you where you can stay." He walked past me, and I got a smell of the cologne he wore, the scent reminding me of when we lived together, of all the memories I shared with him.

I missed him.

I loved him.

I followed Beckham down the hallway, looking to my left as we passed the bathroom, and to my right were two smaller bedrooms. The room he took me to was at the end of the hall on the left, and he pushed the door open and stepped aside, letting me walk in.

This house had been one of the rentals his father owned, one of three properties they had before his father married my mom. I wasn't surprised Beckham now lived in one of them.

"You've really made this house nice, Beckham," I found myself saying and then snapped my mouth shut, my jaw aching from how hard I clenched it. I didn't want to pretend things could be pleasant between us, but I also reminded myself he didn't have to help me. He didn't have to give me a place to stay. He could have told me to fuck off. He didn't even have to answer the damn phone when I called.

I looked over at him when he didn't say anything and saw that he watched me intently. I wondered what he was thinking, wondered if he regretted inviting me to stay.

"I promise I won't be here that long." God, I was so nervous.

He shook his head slowly. "Lenora, I meant it when I said it's not a problem. You're welcome to stay here as long as you want." His voice was soft, gentle. He sounded sincere.

I wanted to believe him, but I was on guard, had

that wall up around me. I kept telling myself this was temporary, that once I had my shit together, I'd be out of his life and hopefully be able to put him in my rearview mirror, so to speak.

I'd be able to put the way I felt for him, the love I felt for him, behind me.

But even thinking that, telling myself that, I knew it was a damn lie.

Beckham

I STOOD on the other side of her bedroom door that I'd just closed, staring at it, picturing her getting settled in there. God, I'd fucked up so badly, but now was my chance to make it right. I didn't want her to leave. Ever. But how could I tell Lenora that? How could I prove to her that I'd loved her for as long as I could remember?

Because she'd throw it back in my face that if somebody loved another person, they never would've said such hurtful things.

My heart fucking broke at that thought.

I exhaled and curled my hands around the door-frame, hanging my head. I couldn't hear anything, and I wondered if she knew I still stood out here. I was seconds away from knocking on the door, but I dug my nails against the wood, telling myself I needed to go slow.

All I wanted to do was talk to her. I could see she was having a hard time. I'd heard it in her voice, not only when she called me and asked for help, but this entire time, with every word she said. Her darkness had come through so strong. And I knew she hit rock-bottom, because she asked for my help. And I was the last person she'd turn to after... everything.

I turned and forced myself to head into the kitchen and opened the freezer, grabbing the bottle of whiskey then getting two shot glasses out of the cupboard. I set the three items on the counter and just stared at them, wondering if going and talking to her right now was the best option. I should let her get settled. We had a lot of things to discuss. I had a lot of things I needed to make amends for.

I put the shot glasses back and took the bottle of whiskey into my room, closing the door and sitting on the edge of my bed. Knowing she was in the room right across the hall had my pulse racing. So instead of making an ass out of myself, I opened up the lid and brought the bottle to my mouth, taking a long drink.

Nothing like getting shitfaced while the girl you were in love with was right across the hall, hating you.

CHAPTER FOUR

Lenora

The next morning

I'D BEEN awake for God knew how long. I'd just stayed in my room, in the bed, staring at the ceiling, watching as light moved through the blinds to cast shadows across the wall.

The truth was, I was nervous. I was scared to face Beckham and this new day, terrified to face my actual reality. Since coming to his home and getting settled in the room, I pretty much stayed to myself. It was only when I heard him ask me through the door if I needed anything from the store and that he'd be back soon that I finally left the room and explored a little.

Although I'd been in this house before when I was younger, helping Beckham and his father paint when they were renting it out, everything was different. Leather furniture adorned the living room, and new granite countertops were in the kitchen. He got rid of the ugly lighting in the dining room, this god-awful '70s-style chandelier that hung over the table that we both used to make fun of. Now in its place was this modern, sleek chrome lighting fixture. In fact, he renovated just about everything in this place.

The bathrooms were redone, with no more gold-leaf mirrors nor Formica countertops. He got rid of all the nasty brown shag-like carpet, replacing it with hardwood flooring. It was gorgeous. I was envious.

The upstairs was a wreck though, with ladders and paint cans. He was renovating that, the loft style area, bedroom, and bathroom upstairs the only rooms above.

And after I grabbed something quick to eat a, I locked myself back in the room for the rest of the day. He hadn't bothered me when he'd gotten home either. Maybe he'd know I needed my space. Maybe he'd know this was just as weird for me as it was for him. Either way, I knew I was going to have to face him... face this new reality eventually.

I might as well get it done and over with, right?

So I pushed the blankets off my body and sat up, letting my feet hang down, my toes touching the bare floor. It was chilly despite this time of year. I braced my hands on the edge of mattress and stared at the window. The blinds were closed, so I couldn't make out what was happening outside, but I imagined how active it would get as the day progressed. People going to work, getting ready to start their day.

Which reminded me that I needed to look for a new job right away. I needed to start making money so I could contribute to staying here, as well as saving up so I could leave. God, I wish I'd had the kind of relationship where I could speak with my mother, where I could lean on her for support, where she told me everything would be okay.

My cell phone vibrated with an incoming text and I glanced over at it, picking it up and looking down at the screen. Speak of the devil. My mother, although I'd like to think her intentions were good, had always been self-absorbed. Her looks, the way she dressed, how she lived in general... it all screamed "Me."

And so when I saw the text picture of the five new designer dresses she had sprawled out across her silk comforter on her king-sized bed, I felt annoyance. Her text explained how she was excited she and Rodney—the man she had the affair with and former student—were attending a charity event at a local country club. She had the nerve to ask me which dress she should wear. My mother, who knew how bad I had it right now, all but rubbed this in my face. My mother, who hadn't even offered to give me moral support, let alone any financial help, sent me this.

All I could do was exhale in frustration and set the phone down.

She didn't care about my problems, because me telling her anything, confiding in her, would only ruin her day. In fact, it had when I explained my job loss, the fact that I couldn't afford my apartment. She'd asked me what I had done wrong to be fired.

She'd actually asked me that.

I ran a hand over my face, rubbing the sleep from my eyes, and slid my fingers through my hair, trying to detangle the strands. I stood and walked over to my bag, grabbing my makeup bag and a change of clothes, and then just stood there and stared at the door.

I didn't hear anything.

"Stop being a baby. You're twenty-two years old, a grown-ass woman. Just get it done and over with.

Don't let him know you're still hurting or that you love him, and you'll be fine." I pulled my shoulders back and held my head high, feeling a little bit of resolve fill me. "Wear that fucking armor like you own it," I whispered to myself, even if I felt like it was a lie right now.

After changing my clothes, I opened the bedroom door, stood there, and just listened. The only thing I could hear was a clock ticking in the distance. All the lights were off, the morning sun illuminating what I could see in the living room, as well as a little bit of the hallway. I stepped out and my bare toes kicked something on the ground. I looked down and saw my favorite candy bar sitting there.

I nearly cried.

He'd gotten it for me when he'd gone to the store.

I bent down, picked it up, and saw some writing on the white package.

These always made you feel better, and I think right now you could really use some cheering up.

Beckham had written that? He felt that way? It seemed like the old him, the man I'd grown up with, the man I fell in love with. But it didn't seem like the man from six months ago.

I didn't want to think too deeply on any of that.

I set the chocolate bar on the nightstand and headed to the bathroom, putting on a little makeup before storing my stuff and going into the kitchen. What I wanted was a big cup of coffee to help me wake up and get my day started, to help me get the motivation to start looking for work. As I saw the coffee machine, I told myself, *fuck it,* and went over to it to start making a pot.

As the coffee brewed, I leaned against the counter and stared out the window. The kitchen and dining room were all one large area, with a decent-sized picture window right in front of the table. The blinds were open slightly, and I could see the neighborhood through them, a woman walking her dog, two elderly ladies speed-walking in nearly identical track suits.

It didn't take much time for the scent of coffee to fill the kitchen, and I grabbed a mug and poured myself some, filling it to the brim. I opened up the fridge, hoping he had half-and-half or at least milk. The latter was all I found, so I opened it and put a little splash in, found the sugar and added a couple spoonsful, then leaned against the counter again and took that first heavenly drink.

I went back to staring out the window. In this

moment, where it was just me, the silence stretching out, I felt peaceful, almost at rest. But that was short-lived when I heard a rustling from down the hallway, then a door opening, then heavy footsteps coming closer.

Instinctually, my body straightened, tightened. I cupped the coffee mug in both hands, felt the warmth through the ceramic, the heat coming through. And then I saw Beckham walk around the corner, his focus on the ground as he ran his hand over the back of his head, slightly messing up the short dark strands.

My heart jumped into my throat at the fact that he only wore a pair of gray sweats and nothing else.

His chest was on full display, toned and defined, hairless and so masculine.

And then my gaze dipped down to his crotch before I could stop myself. I could see the very defined outline of what he sported behind that cotton, and even though he wasn't aroused, his dick was incredibly impressive.

Oh, God.

I felt my entire body heat, flushing. I looked away, because I knew my face had to be red. My heart was racing, my palms starting to sweat, which had nothing to do with the fact that I held a hot cup of coffee.

He glanced up, and I could see he was startled by my presence. He stopped, both of us just staring at the other, that thickness I felt yesterday increasing.

"Hey," he said in a deep voice.

I forced myself not to keep checking him out. It was the last thing I needed on my mind. "Good morning," I said softly, maybe too softly to sound normal. I cleared my throat and gestured to the coffee machine. "I hope it's okay. I made a pot."

He gave me a crooked smile, and I felt my heart jump to my throat. "Lenora, you're welcome to use anything here. You're staying in the house, so what's mine is yours, okay?" He smiled again. "You're hungry—grab whatever you want. You're thirsty—drink the last beer in the fridge. Hell, you want to bake a cake at midnight, have at it."

I actually felt myself chuckle at the last part. "Bake a cake? When have you ever known me to not burn something?"

He started laughing and lifted his hand again to rub the back of his head, giving me a half shrug. "True, but I guess my point is, you're staying here, so this is your home now too."

I didn't know how I felt or how I was supposed to

feel at hearing him say that, but the truth was it had electricity moving through my body. In this one moment, it felt like how we used to be.

It made me feel good hearing him say those things. It made me feel like maybe he didn't hate me. Although I know that was probably not the case, it was a nice passing thought.

Because going down that rabbit hole had my thoughts going darker, that hurt starting to try to creep forward. But I pushed that bitch down. There was no place for that here. Not now. Not ever again.

He came into the kitchen, and I stepped aside so he could grab some coffee. The awkwardness was heavy, so I moved to the dining room table and sat down, staring out the window. I felt Beckham watching me then and glanced over at him.

"You know we need to talk," he finally said, and I exhaled.

"I know." I brought the mug to my mouth and took a long drink. "Just not now," I murmured.

He nodded. "Okay." He sat down across from me, and as we drank our coffee in silence, as I thought about everything that would have to be said, have to be done, this little sliver of hope surfaced in me.

I loved this man. I loved him so much my heart broke in two at the thought of never having him in my life. My heart fucking cracked at knowing what had been lost.

And I felt my world shift in the worst possible way at knowing he'd probably never feel the same way for me as I did for him.

And because of that, I wanted to repair what had been damaged. Because having him in my life, even as just a friend, was better than not having him at all.

I just didn't know if that was possible.

CHAPTER FIVE

Beckham
Several days later

SHE'D BEEN AVOIDING me like the fucking plague. And I'd let her. I'd given her space.

But the time for us to talk, to hash things out, lay everything bare, was here.

So I rented us a movie, one we'd seen years ago, a cheesy comedy, but it brought back a lot of good memories. I bought a six-pack of the beer I knew she liked, this peach-flavored one I was never fond of, but because Lenora enjoyed it, I got it. I also ordered us two pizzas, one of them having sausage, ham, and black olives with thin crust just like she liked.

I wanted to bring back those memories we had

together, happy ones, ones that would remind her what we used to have. Maybe I was trying too hard to convince myself that things could go back to the way they'd been, that I hadn't really fucked everything up.

I knew she found a job, and although she'd been avoiding me, I overheard her on the phone with the initial interview. I asked her about it, and that's when she said she got a position at the artisanal café in town. She'd been very excited about it, although she hid it pretty well. But I'd been able to see it on her face... relief. I couldn't help but think it was because she couldn't wait to leave, to get away from me.

And I hated that.

I ran a hand over my jaw as I sat on the couch, waiting for the pizza to arrive. I knew she'd be home in the next twenty minutes, the café closing at six, and because it was just in town, a short ten-minute drive from where we lived, it would take her no time at all to get home.

I'd offered to pick her up, but Lenora had always been really independent, not wanting to rely on anyone else. It was a trait I loved about her, admired.

I thought about having this home with Lenora, sharing it, both of us in the same space together.

God, that sounded so fucking perfect. I wanted to make that my reality, my future forever.

A handful of minutes later, there was a knock on the front door. The pizza. After paying the delivery guy and bringing the boxes into the kitchen, I opened up the fridge and grabbed a beer. It wasn't the kind she liked, but I needed a little something to take the edge off. I was nervous, so fucking terrified of how this conversation would go. I wanted her to tell me about everything that happened, not just hash out the past, but why she called me for help, how the circumstances of the situation brought her back into my life.

I wanted to know all of that so I could try to help fix things. God, that's all I wanted to do... fix things for her, for us.

I popped the cap on the bottle and downed half the beer before I even took a breath. I wasn't the type of man to get nervous about much, but this situation... this right here scared the fucking shit out of me.

And then I heard a car pull into the driveway. She'd called a car service, something I didn't like, something I tried to help her with as well. I wanted to take her to work as often as I could, but she refused any help I offered. She needed a vehicle, but

I knew she couldn't afford it on her own. That was another thing I needed to help her with.

A few moments later, the front door opened and closed. I knew if I didn't intercept her, she'd haul ass down the hallway and into the bedroom, and I wouldn't see her the rest of the night.

"Lenora?" I called out loudly so I made sure she heard. A second later, she popped her head around the corner, looking at me.

"Hey," she said softly.

I cleared my throat and gave her what was no doubt an awkward smile. "How was work?"

She stepped fully into the kitchen, and I could see on the white button-down shirt she wore there was a small coffee stain. Hell, I could smell the scent of vanilla beans and cinnamon on her. Her hair was a little messy, strands falling around her temples as it had gotten loose from her ponytail. Fuck, she was beautiful the way she looked. She was beautiful all the time.

"It was good," she said genuinely and gave me a smile I knew was real, not forced, not uncomfortable.

I nodded and felt my stomach knot up, felt my muscles tighten as my nerves tried to get the better of me. "I—I thought maybe we could have that talk tonight." I stuttered that first word and felt like a fucking moron. A heavy silence stretched between us, and I wondered if she was thinking of a way to get out of it, thinking of an excuse. Maybe she'd tell me she was too tired. I wouldn't blame her. But I sure as hell hoped she didn't.

Finally, she nodded. "Yeah, I think we should probably have that talk now." She looked down at her shirt and started picking at it. "Let me just get changed, okay?" She glanced up at me and I nodded.

"I figure we can eat first. I ordered some pizza, got that peach beer you really like, even rented that cheesy comedy we watched years ago. You know, the one where the guy has no filter and blurts out anything he thinks?"

She chuckled softly, and I knew she'd been taken right back to that memory, the one where we'd been teenagers sitting on the couch, throwing popcorn at the screen.

And that's what I was going to do tonight. And whether she slapped me, told me to fuck off, or hell, maybe in my wildest dreams forgave me, I was just going to throw everything in and hope for the best.

She headed into her room to change, and I got everything ready, grabbing the pizzas, the beer, and headed into the living room. Hell, I had everything set up for the movie, even popped some fucking popcorn and put extra butter on it like she liked.

I had everything ready to go about an hour ago, even though I didn't know if she'd be up for the idea of hanging out with me. But I was thankful as fuck that she was and so damn excited to spend some time with her.

I didn't know how the conversation would go, but surely it couldn't be as awkward as it currently was between us.

At least I hoped it wasn't. I hoped things would be repaired. I hoped we could be like we were... even if what I really desired was Lenora as mine.

CHAPTER SIX

Lenora

I was thankful Beckham hadn't wanted to talk right away. Instead, we ate pizza, drank beer, and watched the movie we'd seen far too many times over the years. It was nice, comforting, and it brought back so many wonderful memories.

But I knew we needed to talk about the real issue at hand. I knew we were going to have to bring up things that hurt, things that dug at the proverbial open wounds. But maybe it would be therapeutic, beneficial for everybody and everything. Maybe it would help heal us, patch the relationship.

I sure as hell hoped so.

The movie ended, and we sat there in silence for

a few seconds. He was on one end of the couch, and I was on the other, an oversized throw blanket over my legs, which were tucked underneath my bottom. I had one elbow on the arm of the couch and rested my head on my palm. My heart started beating fast, because I knew what was next.

But instead of jumping into that right away, I started in on how my life had gone down the shitter, so to speak.

I was deflecting like hell.

"Long story short, my boss is a sexist, sexual harassment lawsuit walking on two legs, which is ironic, since he's an attorney." I swallowed the disgust I felt. "I was his glorified coffee getter, and when I refused to have sex with him, well, he found some bogus discrepancy and fired me." I rested my head back on the couch and looked up at the ceiling. "Then my roommate told me she was moving in with her boyfriend and not renewing the lease on her place. So I was now homeless. And to make matters worse, my car finally ended up kicking the bucket, and it would have cost more to fix than it was worth." I shrugged. "I didn't have extra funds to repair it anyway." I exhaled, because my story was so fucking depressing it almost didn't even sound real.

"And you couldn't turn to your mom?"

I glanced up at him.

"Not that I wish you had, but it's really fucking sad you couldn't even ask your mom for help."

I shook my head. "I meant it when I said I haven't been speaking with her. She texts me every now and then, oblivious or just ignorant to the fact that she fucked things up. She clearly doesn't see it, but I've all but written her out of my life. It was a long time coming." I sighed and closed my eyes. "I sound like one of those depressing country songs." I snorted, but there was nothing funny about it.

"I'm sorry," he said softly, and I could hear how much he meant those two words. "I'm sorry about you not being able to lean on your mom. I'm sorry that your boss is a dirty motherfucker who needs his teeth kicked in." I looked over at him then. "I'm just really sorry, Lenora."

I shrugged. "It's fine. I'm fine. That's life, I guess." I looked down at my hands, picking at a thread on the blanket. "I'm just glad I could ask you for help." I swallowed roughly. "You were the only person I could turn to, but after... well, after all that, I was terrified but had no other options." I glanced back at my hands, feeling so nervous I could throw up right now.

"Lenora?" He said my name softly.

I looked over at him. The glow from the TV illuminated the darkened living room. The kitchen light was still on, and a soft, white light came from the other side, casting shadows across Beckham.

I thought about our last interaction, the last time we'd been face-to-face six months ago. And thinking about what happened, what was said, pulled me into the past until I felt like I was drowning in it.

I WAS CRYING. So was Beckham. Even his father was sobbing. And my mother, the one person who started this catalyst of pain and hurt, had left, not wanting the "dramatics" of the end of everyone's story.

I looked over at Rob, Beckham's father, and I felt my heart breaking for him. He sat on the couch with his head in his hands, his big body shaking. I'd never seen a grown man cry before, but when my mother's infidelity came to light, when she admitted she no longer loved Rob, that she hadn't been in love with him for a very long time, I literally watched the life fade from his eyes.

He been in love with my mother, that was clear. That was his mistake. It was very obvious he also thought they were going to be together forever, grow old, enjoy family holidays with grandchildren. He had their life mapped out.

I lifted my hand and rubbed my chest, an ache settling there. I looked back at Beckham. He glanced at me like he... hated me.

"Beckham," I said, wanting to tell him none of this was my fault, that none of this was his. It wasn't Rob's or anyone else's. It was my mother's fault, only hers.

God, I was so sorry.

I took a step toward him, but he shook his head, his eyes narrowing as he glanced at his father. I could hear Rob sobbing softly, and when Beckham slid his gaze back over to me, the loathing I knew he felt for my mother in that instant was projected onto me.

"I had no idea." That was the truth. My mother had always been an absentee parent, had never shown me much attention. I hadn't noticed anything different.

"How could you have not?" His voice was like venom, acid over my skin.

I felt my anger grow. "The same way you didn't see it. The same way Rob didn't see it." I saw his jaw clench almost violently.

"She's your mother, Lenora." The way he said my name had my heart stopping for just a second. He sounded like he didn't know me.

"Beckham, you're hurting. But please don't take it out on me." When I'd come home, everyone was fighting, yelling, insults being thrown out. That's when I

heard Beckham slighting my mother. That's when I snapped.

All I saw was my mother with wide eyes looking between them, once again playing the victim. And I'd instantly gotten defensive. She might've been a shitty mom, but all I saw was the woman who'd given me life. And I guess that was my mistake.

Beckham had called her a whore, and something in me had defended her, screamed at him. It had been a rant, like this instinct to protect her, even if I didn't know if she'd do the same for me. All I thought was... that's my mom.

The dramatics of it all consumed me so much that I felt like I couldn't breathe. I called him hateful, disrespectful, asked him who the fuck he thought he was. I did all this before I heard the entire story. And all the while, my mother stood back, not saying one word. And then she was gone, muttering about the dramatics and not wanting anything to do with us, grumbling how she was glad things were finally out in the open.

And it was only after she left that I found out the whole story.

"Your mother is disgusting, Lenora. An unfaithful bitch," Beckham said, his voice cracking from emotion.

"Stop it," I begged, pleaded.

"Look at what she's done to my father!" His voice was

hard, hateful. He tipped his chin toward his dad, who still sat on the couch. "Look at what the fuck she's done to him, Lenora. And you wanted to defend her? You wanted to defend her without knowing the full story?" He shook his head slowly, his eyes narrowing even more, this hard- ness moving across his face.

"You're hurting. I understand. But please don't do or say anything you're going to regret later." I probably shouldn't have said the latter, but the words were already out, and I watched as his eyes widened ever-so-slightly before he regained his composure.

His jaw clenched, and he took a step back, slowly shaking his head as if he couldn't believe what was going on. I couldn't believe what was going on either. The family was broken up. It was like I was thrown into this nightmare where everything I'd ever known was being ripped away from me.

"Do something I'll regret?" He scoffed. "I already have by being part of your family."

My heart hurt something fierce in that moment, at that comment.

"You're just like her," he said, and I felt the tears rush up. He knew how my mother was, how she'd been with me, and the fact that he said that cut me deep. "You want things to be smoothed over, things to go back to the way they were?"

I opened my mouth but snapped it closed, unsure what to say, unsure what I could say. The tears were already falling, because I knew where this was going. "You're just like her, Lenora. It's best that we will never have to see each other again, because looking at you only reminds me of her and what she did to my father. Looking into your blue eyes does nothing but piss me off and make me hate you."

I felt like I'd been transferred to some different dimension, where this wasn't the Beckham I'd always known.

"Come on, Dad," Beckham said and curled his lip as he looked at me. "Let's get the fuck out of here and get a beer. There's nothing for us here anymore. Maybe there never was."

And as he and his father started leaving, I found myself walking toward them and reaching out, taking hold of Beckham's wrist and forcing him to stop. He looked over his shoulder at me, and all I saw was... nothing. Absolutely nothing reflected back at me.

"Beckham." My voice hitched. "I don't even know what's going on right now. Please don't leave."

I felt the dejection from him, the distance. He pulled his arm away from me as if I'd burned his skin. "Just stay away from us," Beckham said with so much hatred I couldn't keep myself from crying out, the tears a steady flow down my cheeks.

"Beckham," I whispered. What in the hell was going on right now?

The way he looked at me... it was as if he stared at the one person who ruined everything. My mother. He saw her in me. In this moment, I knew he was blinded by the hurt and betrayal, and I was the easiest target.

"AH, FUCK, LENORA," Beckham said, pulling me back to the present and from my thoughts.

I realized I'd totally disconnected right then and there. I felt the tears sliding down my cheeks and quickly brushed them away. He moved closer, and I took a stuttering breath.

"You broke my heart, Beckham," I finally admitted. I'd never spoken those words out loud.

He was by me a second later, embracing me. I didn't stop him, didn't push him away.

"I know," was all he said, his arms wrapped tightly around me as he pulled me impossibly closer. "I fucked up so badly, Lenora. So badly." His words were so soft I almost didn't hear them. "I fucked up."

CHAPTER SEVEN

Beckham

GOD, I'd forever regret how I hurt her.

I was the reason she was like this, crying, her body leaning against mine, the desperation and sadness in her voice all because of me. And it had taken her contacting me and six long damn months for me to try to rectify this. But she wasn't pushing me away, didn't tell me to fuck off. She let me hold her, and God it felt incredible.

I didn't know how long we sat there, her leaning against my chest, seeking support, comfort, my arms around her body, listening to her start to calm down. But I'd hold her forever if that's what it took, if that's what she wanted.

It was only then that I pulled back slightly, looking into her face. I didn't stop myself from lifting my hand and running my thumb across her cheek, wiping away her tears. I wanted to kiss them away. I wanted to be the man who made sure she never felt like this ever again.

"I'm so damn sorry, Lenora." Those words seemed so inadequate, so insignificant and tame in comparison to how I actually felt. "I regretted what I said as soon as it came from my mouth, as soon as I saw the hurt I caused you. I didn't mean one goddamn fucking word I said that day."

She wiped the remaining wetness off her cheeks and nodded, but she wasn't meeting my gaze. "Why didn't you ever reach out to me? Why didn't you ever contact me if you were so sorry?"

I didn't know what to say. But I couldn't leave her wondering, couldn't let that question hang between us. "Stupidity. Embarrassment." I cleared my throat. "I picked up my phone so many times, Lenora. So. Many. Times. I wanted to call you. I've driven by your place more times than I can count, more times than I even want to admit. But in the end, it was fear that kept me away."

She looked up at me then, and I saw the confusion on her face. "Fear?" She exhaled slowly, and I waited for her to continue, because honestly I had no idea what else to say. I didn't know what to say or do to make things right. "Why would you possibly be afraid to reach out to me?"

It was my turn to exhale as I shifted on the couch and leaned against the cushion, putting a little bit of distance between us so she could breathe, so she didn't feel like I was crowding her. "Because I was sure I had done irreparable damage. For the last six months, all I've done is think about what I said to you, how I looked at you. None of that was your fault. I projected my anger for your mother, the hurt I knew my father felt, onto you. I'd seen my father's heart break, and because you were there, trying to reach out to me, trying to make things better... I just lashed out." I felt so many emotions right now. So many they were drowning me. "And I've regretted it every fucking minute of every day since then, Lenora." My chest hurt, my heart aching. I lifted my hand and rubbed my sternum, wanting nothing more than to pull her close and embrace her.

She felt incredible when I held her, and I wanted to keep that feeling, to bottle it up for when I felt like shit. I could draw upon it and feel like a brand-new man.

"But I was humiliated. I hurt you so deeply that I

knew you'd never speak to me again, so when you called me, it was like fate was giving me another chance, like destiny had put us in each other's lives once more." I ran my hand over my hair, lightly tugging at the strands at my nape. I was frustrated with myself. I hated myself. "But that's not an excuse. I shouldn't have waited so long. I shouldn't have been too afraid, too embarrassed to call you. I should've made things right as soon as I said that crap to you." I looked into her eyes deeply, wanting her to see how true and genuine my words really were. "But listen to me, Lenora. Listen as closely as you've ever listened to anyone before." My heart was in my throat, beating wildly, fast, and franticly. "Whatever it takes, whatever I have to do for the rest of my fucking life, I will make it up to you. I will make things right."

I heard her breath hitch and wondered what she thought. She had every right to slap me, to curse me out. I wouldn't blame her. I'd welcome it, because I deserved it. I deserved her hatred and her loathing, but God, I didn't want any of it. I just wanted her.

So I just said it, laid my cards all out there.

"Because I love you, Lenora. I've loved you for years."

The smile she gave me was soft, sweet. "I love you too, Beckham."

I'd wanted—dreamed—of her saying those words to me, to say she was in love with me. But I knew the love she felt for me wasn't the kind I had for her, that I fantasized about. And that was okay. Because I would take Lenora in my life anyway I could get her.

"Will you forgive me? Can you ever forgive me?" She was silent for a long time, so long that I thought maybe she'd never answer, fearing that when she finally did say something, it would be the opposite of what I desperately needed to hear.

"That's all I've ever wanted to hear for six months, Beckham. I should hate you, never speak to you again, but I can't. I love you too much."

We stared into each other's eyes, and I didn't stop myself from reaching out and pulling her in close, burying my face in the crook of her neck, closing my eyes, and just inhaling deeply

She smelled good, like my happiness and memories that wrapped up in this euphoric sensation I always felt when I was with her.

"I love you so fucking much, Lenora. Not seeing you or talking to you this half a year has been hell. And I only have myself to blame."

She wrapped her arms around me, and I shuddered, my body shaking slightly, because it felt so damn good to have her close.

"I love you too, Beckham."

I was a big man, strong and powerful. I wasn't afraid of anything, didn't back down when challenged. Men were afraid of me, because I had confidence, because I didn't let anyone fuck me over. But this woman... this woman could bring me to my knees faster than anything else on this planet. Only this woman had any kind of power over me.

I leaned back and cupped her cheek, smoothing my thumb right under her eye, feeling how smooth her skin was, how warm she was. I dipped my gaze down to her lips, not wanting to cross lines but feeling so vulnerable and bare right now that I couldn't stop myself.

"Do you know what I mean when I say I love you, Lenora?" I asked softly and tore my gaze from her mouth to look into her eyes. I saw her pupils dilate, heard her breathing increase. Was it arousal? Was it shock? Either way, she didn't push me away. She let me hold her, touch her. "Do you *really* know what I mean when I say I love you?" She shook her head slowly, although I could see the lie in her expression. She knew. "It's not the way I should love you, probably. But I can't stop myself."

She took in a stuttering breath. "Beckham?" Her voice was so soft I almost didn't hear her say my name.

"And I know you're probably wondering how I could say those awful things to you when I'm madly in love with you. How could I have hurt you the way I did, when you're the only woman I want?" I swallowed the thick lump in my throat. She didn't say anything, but her expression spoke loudly. What I said penetrated her deeply. I ran a hand over my jaw, feeling a day's worth of stubble covering it. "And I don't have an answer to that. All I can say is it was in the heat of the moment, my father's pain consuming me. I lashed out at the wrong person. God, Lenora. I am so fucking sorry. That day will be the biggest fucking mistake of my life. My one regret." I looked into her eyes, pleading without saying anything in that moment. "And I don't need you to love me back. I just need you to be in my life. I'll take whatever I can get." I was desperate for her friendship, for her in my life.

I just hoped it wasn't too late.

CHAPTER EIGHT

Lenora

I WANTED to kiss him so badly.

I wanted him to kiss me more than anything in the world in that moment.

But I was confused—the situation, the emotions I felt, so profound I couldn't breathe. I felt dizzy, scared.

I was excited and aroused.

I found myself breaking away from him and standing, unable to form words, unable to say anything in that moment.

I couldn't even breathe.

"Beckham—I...." I didn't even know what to say.

The revelation, truth he'd just given me, rocked my world.

So instead of saying something wrong, awkward, or putting my foot in my mouth, I walked away from him. I made my way into the kitchen, finally able to suck in a breath, to try to gather my thoughts.

He loves me.

Beckham's in love with me.

I braced my hands on the counter, curling my fingers around the granite, the stone cold, hard... sturdy and keeping me upright in that moment.

I closed my eyes and breathed out. I didn't know how long I stood there; it could've been hours for all I knew but in reality was probably just mere seconds. I heard Beckham come into the kitchen, could feel the heaviness come from him in what he wanted to say. But he stayed silent until I turned around and faced him.

The way he looked at me was like a broken man, so much pain and anguish coming from him that all I wanted to do was go up to Beckham and embrace him. But right now, I shouldn't worry about the past. I shouldn't worry about anything but what he said to me, what he confided in me.

He was in love with me.

I could've prolonged this, questioned how he

could have said those hurtful things to me if he'd been in love with me. Maybe it didn't make any sense; maybe I shouldn't believe a word he said. But I did. I looked into his face, stared into his eyes, and I knew the truth.

He was truly sorry.

He truly regretted what he said and what happened.

He didn't mean any of it.

And he was in love with me.

I played that last bit over and over in my mind, grasping for it like it wasn't my reality.

"I'm sorry," he said softly. "I shouldn't have brought any of this up," he said and exhaled, looking down at his feet as if he regretted the situation.

But I didn't want him to. I was letting it slowly sink in. I was coming to terms with the reality of how my life was forever changing. And that's why I'd walked away. That's why I left Beckham sitting in the living room by himself.

Because I had to process this.

But my reality wasn't for the worse this time. It was absolutely for the better.

"Beckham," I finally said, and he looked up at me instantly. "I'm in love with you too," I admitted for the first time in my life, actually saying those words out loud. I'd felt them, thought them for so long that they'd been a part of me, buried so deep it was almost as if I had drowned in them.

And they were out in the open now, hanging between us.

I heard him suck in a breath, his expression telling me he was shocked to hear me say I was in love with him too.

"I'm just so confused," I whispered the truth. My truth. Before I knew what was happening, he was in front of me, his hands on either side of my face, his big palms engulfing my cheeks.

He tipped my head back so I could look at him, but he said nothing. Neither did I. This moment was very profound, very healing.

I felt it down to my bones.

It was like that wound I had for so long was finally closing, was finally getting better. And so I did something I never thought I'd ever do in my life.

I did something that took a lot of courage.

I did something I was proud of myself for.

I rose up on my toes and kissed him.

CHAPTER NINE

Lenora

THE KISSED STARTED OFF SLOW, tentative, but as the seconds moved by, I felt something in Beckham shift, snap.

He was the one kissing me now.

His motions were feverish, like an animal had been unleashed inside him. I felt my arousal grow, my excitement climb. I couldn't breathe, could only *feel* him.

"I'm sorry," he murmured but still kissed me. "I should go slow," he whispered against my mouth, but I pressed my body harder against his.

I'd never done anything like this with a man, nothing remotely sexual. I focused on school, work. I focused on making sure I could have a good life. Boys hadn't been in that equation at a young age.

But when I felt desire and arousal, the only person who had ever come into my thoughts was the man currently kissing me.

"Don't stop," I whispered back.

"Never." He groaned out that lone word.

I felt how hard he was as he moved closer, his erection digging against my belly. I might be a virgin, but I wasn't a prude. I knew what happened during sex, on how these things progressed. I went to a public school, heard the way guys spoke about it, saw movies. But I was still so nervous.

I felt him grind himself against my stomach over and over again, and I found myself moaning into his mouth. He swallowed the sound greedily.

"I've wanted this for so long," he said in a breathless tone. "So long."

And as I stared into his face, this little part of me cried out with joy.

"I love you, Beckham."

He closed his eyes and rested his forehead on mine. For long seconds, neither of us said anything. Then he pulled me close and just held me.

"You have no idea what it does to me to know

you love me too, that you don't hate me. That you can forgive me."

I closed my eyes and just breathed in and out. "I do forgive you." And I did. This intense heat filled me. I grew wet between my legs, my entire body lighting up for Beckham. He ran a hand over my back, up and down, slow and easy. But that gentle touch did something wicked to me, had me wanting things I'd only ever dreamed of before, not with anyone but Beckham.

I knew where this was headed, and I wasn't going to try to rationalize that this might ruin what we were trying to build and accomplish with moving past the... well, the past. I wouldn't allow myself to be afraid of the "what ifs" anymore.

This felt right, so I was going to jump in head first and see if I landed whole on the other side.

"I love you, Beckham," I said again and heard him groan.

"Lenora. God. I feel like I've hit the jackpot, not just with your forgiveness, but because of everything else. The way you look at me... your love."

I pulled back and looked into his face. I saw the way he looked at my mouth, could feel his need for me. It was as potent as mine for him.

"It's always been you for me, Lenora, even if I never said it, even if you never knew."

My breath caught at his words.

"There was never a moment where my love for you was questioned. Not even when I was a total jackass and said those fucking awful things. Never, baby. Never." He stroked my cheek with his thumb. "You're the only one I love, the only one I'll ever love." When he lifted his gaze to my eyes, my heart jumped into my throat. "Hell, Lenora, I've never even been with a woman, because I only wanted you."

I didn't know what to say in that moment, didn't know how to react.

Beckham was a virgin? Like me? How was that even possible? How could a man so attractive, so sexually potent, be innocent like I was? God, it didn't seem real, because his reasoning for never having sex was because of... *me*?

"W-what?" I stuttered that one word out.

In my head, I screamed out for him to kiss me, to hold me, to tell me he loved me over and over again. But I couldn't find the words.

Beckham moved his thumb along my skin in slow, gentle sweeps. "I'm a virgin, Lenora. No other woman ever interested me. No other woman has ever been able to hold a candle to you."

"To know you're mine, that you want me too...." His big body shuddered.

Is this really happening?

My heart was in my throat, and I found myself lifting my arms and curling my hands around his biceps. His flesh was warm, smooth, and I curled my fingers gently into his skin even more. The sleeves of his white T-shirt rose up, and I realized it was because I was slowly inching my hands up.

"I know what I feel for you, what we have had throughout the years, is the realest thing I've ever experience, Lenora." His expression was so intense in that moment. "You're the realist thing in my life, and I won't let you go."

"Be with me, Beckham," I whispered, those words spilling from me before I could stop them. I felt him playing with the hair by my ear, and chills raced up my spine. I'd thought about this moment plenty of times, fantasized that this would be my reality. I never thought it would ever happen though.

He looked at my mouth again, and I felt the tips of his fingers brush along the side of my neck. Every part of me was on fire. I parted my mouth and sucked in a breath, the act involuntary, unavoidable.

He moved impossibly closer, but I wanted him

pressed right up against me, wanted there to be no denying we were here and about to do this.

"Be with you, Lenora?" He swallowed, and I heard how rough it sounded, like he was nervous.

I nodded.

"Are you sure about that, baby?" His voice was whisper-soft.

I looked right into his eyes. "I've never been surer of anything in my life, Beckham. Take me to your room."

CHAPTER TEN

Beckham

GOD, I'd never felt such intense emotions as I did right now. It wasn't even about sex or arousal, or any of those physical sensations racing through my body. It was the fact that this girl, this woman, loved me the same way I loved her. I'd fantasized about this moment plenty of times, but never in my life did I think it could be my reality.

We were in my room now. After she told me those words, I all but lifted her off the ground and carried her here. No, with the door shut and the woman I loved right in front of me, I knew I was never going to let her go.

Not only did Lenora love me the way I loved her,

but I could feel what was about to happen. I could sense her arousal for me, her need for me. It matched my own, and mine was pretty fucking intense.

"Lenora," I groaned. "Baby, I want to kiss you so damn badly." I hadn't meant to just blurt that out.

She licked her lips and I held in my groan. "If you don't, I will."

My heart hiccuped at her words.

I looked at her pink, full lips and wanted to get lost in the sensation of our mouths pressed together, of my body against hers, of everything I'd ever dreamed about with Lenora coming full circle. I wanted to kiss her until neither one of us could breathe, until we were gasping for air... until she was clutching at me for more.

Something in me broke as I slammed my mouth down on hers, this wild beast inside of me coming free, tearing at the surface.

She gasped against my mouth and held onto me as I fucked her with my tongue and lips, as I devoured her, took her taste into my body. My dick was stiff, hard like steel. I ached for her, to see how tight and wet she was, to feel how hot she was.

She wound her arms around my neck and rose on her toes so she was totally flush with me. My cock jerked behind my jeans, but I wanted more. So much more. Lenora dug her nails into my nape, and I hissed out in pleasure and pain. I wanted more of that.

"I need you so fucking badly," I said. I walked her backward until the bed stopped our movements. I tangled my hands around her hair, tugging at the strands, tilting her head back slightly. And as I kissed her over and over again, I felt high, drunk... dazed.

"Don't stop," Lenora gasped against my mouth.

"Never," I promised. I thrust my tongue into her mouth, this guttural sound leaving me. I used my other hand to span her lower back, pulling her even closer so she could see how hard she made me.

I stroked my tongue along hers and then pulled hers deeper into my mouth. I found myself pressing my dick against her belly, humping her, thrusting my aching cock back and forth to relieve some of the pressure. I pulled back only long enough to groan, "No other guy will touch you, Lenora." I stared into her eyes until she nodded, agreeing with me. "There's no way I could stand any other asshole even looking at you with desire."

"Good," she whispered, her lips red and glossy

from my kiss. "Because I've never wanted anyone but you."

I crushed her to me again, speared both my hands into her hair, and kissed her until we were both gasping for air, until the wet, sloppy, and sexual sounds of us making out surrounded us.

I mouth fucked her.

She arched into me, her breasts pressing into my chest, letting me feel how hard her nipples were. Damn, I wanted her naked, wanted her bare chest right up against mine. My cock jerked again like a motherfucker at that thought.

If I didn't get some control, this would be over before it even started, and no way in hell would I be one of those guys who shot his load before things really got started. But having Lenora here made it almost impossible to rein in that control.

Almost.

Burying my face in her neck, I inhaled deeply, getting intoxicated from the way she smelled. *God. So good.*

"Take me, Beckham. Take me now," she whispered.

And then we were on the bed, Lenora's back to the mattress, my body covering hers. It felt right, perfect. Before I could comprehend what she was doing, Lenora had her top lifted and pulled over her head. And then I was staring at her breasts. The fact that she was braless had my entire body tightening. My dick jerked fiercely, and I felt my balls draw up tight. I could have come from the sight of her.

"*Christ*, baby." I found myself lowering my head and resting it on her chest, feeling how warm she was, smelling the clean sweat that started to cover her skin, because she was getting so worked up for me.

She smelled good, clean like lemons and soap, crisp like the fucking winter air when the wind picked up. It turned me on even more, pre-cum lining the tip of my cock. God, I was going to fill her up so much my seed would slip out of her. I'd rub it into her skin, marking her, making her smell like me.

I wanted to be so deep inside Lenora there was no doubt in her mind that she was mine.

"Beckham," she groaned as if she were in desperate need of only what I could give her. I immediately started undoing the button of my jeans then pulled the zipper down. I forced myself to stop as I looked at her. "You're sure about this, baby?"

She nodded right away, and I bit my tongue to

hold off the sound of need that would have come from me.

"Yes," she moaned. "I've always wanted this." She worked off her bottoms and panties, and I shifted on the bed to finish getting undressed. Then we were both naked, my gaze roaming over her perfect body. She was thick and curvy in all the right places. I was frozen in place as I stared at the creamy, perfect flesh that covered her from head to toe, as I memorized every part of her. Never in my wildest dreams could I have imagined she'd be so fucking incredible.

"Spread your legs, baby," I said in the must guttural voice I ever heard come from me. And when she did what I wanted, I felt my mouth water. She was so pink, so wet. The thatch of hair that covered the top of her pretty pussy was trimmed, a deep shade blonde. God... her fucking clit was slightly engorged, ready for me to suck on.

She was like that because of me. All because of me.

I lifted my gaze over her slightly rounded belly, along the indentation of her navel, and stopped when I got to her big, handful-sized breasts. Her nipples were a deep pink, hard, my mouth watering even more for a taste of her.

"I need you," she whispered.

My body burned alive at hearing her say that.

Christ.

"I'll never get enough of you," I said truthfully.

"I need you now," she repeated with more desperation in her tone.

My throat tightened, my desire ready to burn me alive. I groaned. "I should go slow. We should take our time."

She shook her head. "We've done enough of that to last a lifetime."

This woman was my everything, and hearing her say that had this primal need filling me. I wanted this moment to be special for her. But as I stared at her face, I knew that because we were together, it was already so fucking special. I could have easily lost control the moment I kissed her, but I was reining it in. I was trying to go slow for her.

All I could think about was unleashing the passion I'd had for Lenora all these years in the most physical of senses.

And as I stared into her eyes, I knew she was right here with me, wanting that too.

CHAPTER ELEVEN

Lenora

"God, I've never seen anyone or anything as beautiful as you. I never will," Beckham groaned out, his voice deep, slightly gruff.

I shouldn't have checked him out the way I was, so obscene and lewd-like, but there was no helping it. He was all hard muscles and golden skin.

Beckham was rough around the edges, yet smooth enough he could have been called a pretty boy. He was in shape without obsessively trying to be.

And as I let my gaze lower to what he sported down below... all I could do was swallow in appreciation.

He had a massive erection, thick and long, huge and big enough I felt my throat tighten. The crown of his cock was slightly wider than the shaft, and my inner muscles clenched as I imagined him trying to push all of those monstrous inches into my virgin body.

I swallowed hard, this sudden lump in my throat.

"You can't stare at me that way, baby."

I lifted my gaze from his cock and knew my eyes must be wide as saucers.

"Because I'm liable to come just from the fact that you're looking at my dick." His voice was even more guttural now.

"I'm so wet for you," I whispered.

"God, Lenora," he said in this strained whisper. And as I watched him grab his cock, his hand large but not dwarfing it in the slightest, I felt my heart beat even harder.

Every part of me felt hot, with emotions and sensations crashing through me.

And the way he looked at me was like a man dying to have more.

And I was that *more*.

"I want you so fucking badly, Lenora." Hearing him say that sent fire through my veins.

I lifted my hands and ran them up his arms,

feeling his muscles flex under my touch. I was wet, so soaked it felt slippery between my thighs.

And it was all for Beckham. It had always been for him.

He made this low sound deep in his chest, all feral and crazed.

Then his big body covered mine. He had his hands on my chest, his mouth on mine. The way he kissed me had all common sense and rationalization leaving me violently. My legs were spread so damn wide for him, and I felt his cock right on my pussy. He was hot and hard, like velvet over steel.

"I can feel how wet you are for me," he said breathlessly. He licked my bottom lip, and I couldn't hold in the groan that spilled from me. Beckham moved his mouth over my jaw and started sucking at my pulse point right below my ear, running his tongue along my flesh, and gently biting me until my entire body tightened. It felt so good.

He felt so good.

"I'm burning up for you." I couldn't even breathe, let alone think straight. "I need you."

He started pressing his cock against my pussy over and over again, long seconds passing.

My hands were shaking, my passion so potent it was like another person inside me.

Beckham lowered his gaze to my breasts, and I wondered if he took notice at how hard my nipples had become, as if begging for his mouth.

Without saying anything, he leaned forward, his upper body pressing me farther back on the bed. And when I felt his tongue on one of my nipples, I closed my eyes and bit my lip as ecstasy coursed through me.

I heard my heart thundering in my ears, felt it in my throat. I gathered the sheets in my hands, pulled at them, feeling everything in me come alive even more as he alternated between each breast, sucking and licking at the turgid peaks until I shook from how good it all felt.

He moved his mouth over my breasts then lower to my ribs. He continued a downward path to my navel, running his tongue along the indentation, his hands on my waist holding me down, keeping me still. And still, he went lower, over my hipbones, licking, kissing, nipping.

And when I felt his mouth right over my pussy, his hot breath coming in hard, fast pants, I curled my toes in pleasure. I could have climaxed right then and there.

"Yes," I hissed out, even though he hadn't asked

me anything. I wasn't embarrassed it had come out of me so passionately.

I reached up and tangled my hands in his hair, pulling at the strands until Beckham groaned. The way he licked at me, his head between my legs, his tongue running up and down my slit, had me nearly orgasming right then and there.

He latched his mouth over my clit, and I cried out, as that was my tipping point... my breaking point. I came for him so hard I saw stars.

I couldn't think, couldn't even breathe. I pulled at his hair, keeping him against me, needing his mouth right there. I ground my pussy against his face, so wanton in this moment I didn't even feel like myself. But God, it felt good. So good.

Beckham moved his mouth down my cleft to my opening and plunged his tongue in, spreading my lips wide open with his thumbs, fucking me there like I desperately needed him to do with his cock.

"So sweet," he groaned against my soaked, clenching flesh.

When the tremors faded, he moved back up my body and kissed me hard and possessively. I tasted myself on him, a sweet, musky flavor that had my heart racing all over again and had me moaning as I lifted my lower half and rubbed myself on him.

And as I felt him thrust against me over and over again, I knew once he was in me, fucking me, making love to me, neither one of us would be able to walk away.

And I'd never anticipated anything more.

CHAPTER TWELVE

Beckham

Fuck.

There was nothing better, would never be anything better, than having this woman love me.

I wasn't even inside Lenora yet, and already I was trying not to get off. My balls were drawn up to my body, so full of cum for her, and I was having one hell of a time keeping myself in control.

I wanted this to last so badly. I wanted to feel her pussy clenching around my cock, milking me, because she wanted my seed filling her up.

"Beckham," she moaned in the hottest way. "Beckham. I'm so ready for you."

I ran my tongue along her bottom lip, wanting to

mouth fuck her desperately. I was tense, my muscles straining under my skin. My cock was so hard, and I felt pre-cum at the tip. I looked at her face, saw how pink her cheeks were, saw the way her pupils were dilated.

She was so fucking ready for me. So was so damn primed.

I was so possessive of her, and the very thought of any man touching her, talking to her... hell, even looking at her, pissed me off and made me want to mark and claim her over and over again.

She started breathing harder, and I slid my hand between us and ran my finger along her slit. God, she felt like silk. I had my cock aligned at her pussy hole, but I didn't thrust in deep. I waited. I savored.

Fuck. Yes.

I felt how her pussy was hot and soaking for me. I plunged my tongue inside her mouth, forcing her to take it all, fucking her there like I would between her thighs.

I needed my cock in her pussy now, but I waited. I tormented us.

"Baby," I groaned against her mouth, my hips having a mind of their own and wanting to plunge forward, burying my cock inside her tight, virgin heat. And so I got ready to do just that. "Lenora, if I don't get inside of you, I'll come before we can give each other our virginities, and I want to be buried in your tight pussy when we both get off."

She gasped, and I kissed her harder. Lenora ran her tongue along my lip, and my whole body shook in response. "Spread your legs wider for me," I murmured against her mouth.

I knew she was losing control. I could feel it in the tightening of her muscles, the way she mewled for me. And when she was so fucking wide for me her muscles probably protested, I placed the tip of my cock at her entrance.

She arched, pressing her breasts against my chest, and that's when I thrust my hips forward, pushing my cock deeper into her. I had no fucking control right now. It was like I was crazed, delirious for her. Her pussy was so tight, so wet. She was so hot, so primed for me I almost came right then.

Not yet. Keep it the fuck together for her.

"Are you okay?" I managed to grit out, wanting to make sure she wasn't in too much pain.

She moaned and shook her head. "I'm fine. Keep going. Don't stop."

Fuck, I'd never stop.

I was fully seated inside her now, my balls pressed right up against her ass, her pussy clenching around my cock. I started moving in and out of her slowly, gently. My pleasure built... the pressure along with it. The need to stay calm, to make sure this was good for her, was at the forefront of my mind. I hunched my shoulders forward, lowered my head, and claimed her mouth as I thrust in and out of her.

I pulled out and pushed into her especially hard, and she gasped and held on tighter, digging her nails in deeper. She was so fucking primed for me.

"You feel so good." I couldn't stop the words from spilling from my mouth. The feeling of her pussy squeezing my cock and of her wanting this so damn badly made me almost come right then and there.

"I want to be so deep inside you nothing else matters."

"When I'm with you, nothing else matters, Beckham."

Fuck, I felt the exact same. Nothing else mattered but this woman right here.

CHAPTER THIRTEEN

Lenora

I COULDN'T LIE. It hurt losing my virginity. The pain was sudden, breath-stealing. The feeling of Beckham stretching me, filling me to the point I felt like I'd break in two.

But even though it hurt, knowing Beckham was the one with me, taking my innocence, had that discomfort taking a backseat. It had my pleasure rising.

"Are you okay?" he asked softly, and I nodded.

I didn't want to tell him how badly it initially hurt, because what good would that do? So instead, I curled my hands around his biceps a little tighter and whispered, "Don't stop."

The strain on his face was clear, and I knew it was because he was trying to keep his control in check for me.

He thrust in slow and easy, and I swore he was holding his breath. Heat started to build inside of me, that discomfort still there but not as powerful as it had initially been. And as the time passed, I start to felt that bone-deep pleasure that I always thought came with having sex. But I knew it wasn't just the physical aspect of it, but the fact that I was here with Beckham.

He was big and thick, hitting parts of me that had my toes curling and my heart racing. Sweat beaded my brow, my breathing was erratic, and I felt something building deep inside me.

"God, Lenora, you feel so good." Beckham closed his eyes and groaned softly, and that sound had my pulse beating right in my clit. "Grip on to me as I take you, as I claim you and you claim me." He leaned closer to my mouth. "Hold onto me as I make love to you... as I fuck you."

A shiver worked through me, and I couldn't stop myself from gasping at his crude, blunt words. I had my hands on his biceps, my nails digging into his flesh. Beckham started pulling out of me, the tip of his cock lodged in my body before he pushed back in, slow and easy, gentle and thorough.

He buried his face in the crook of my neck again, and I wrapped my arms around him, holding him just as tightly as he held me. He started moving at a steady pace then, in and out, his thick, long cock tunneling through my folds and claiming me.

He hit something deep, and I couldn't hold in my moan.

"Does it feel good, Lenora?" He sounded tense, breathless. I knew he was trying to stay in control for me.

"God. Yes."

He thrust in and out of me slowly and turned his head so he could press his mouth to mine. He filled me, stretched and consumed me, and he was so powerful I couldn't stop my eyes from rolling back in pleasure.

Beckham was hard where I was soft.

When Beckham retreated an inch, the thick head of his cock was poised at my entrance. He stayed still for a second as he stared in my eyes, and then he thrust back in deeply, harder this time. The force of that last push had me shifting up on the mattress. He was almost all the way out again then pushed back into me.

Over and over, he did this, thrusting, pushing, tunneling into me. He moved faster and a little harder with each movement, with each passing second.

"Watch as I take you, Lenora, as I give you my virginity and take yours." He leaned in and kissed me again, grunting. He rose up, braced his hands on the bed by my head, his forearms straight, and looked down the length of our bodies. "God, look at us, baby," he seemed to mutter to himself. I rose up enough that I could watch as he plunged his cock into my pussy. Every time he would retreat, I saw how glossy his shaft was from my pussy, saw the streaks of my virgin blood coating his length.

His head was still downcast, but when I noticed his gaze traveling upward, I tore my focus from where we were connected and stared into his eyes.

"Watching my cock move in and out of you is the hottest fucking thing."

I couldn't agree more.

He went back to watching what was happening between our bodies. He did this for long moments, his movements slow and steady. Easy, as if he were trying to prolong this.

But then he made this low sound in the back of his throat, and I knew he was losing his grip on his control. He had his hands on my waist, his fingers digging into my flesh painfully, pleasurably. Before I knew what was happening, Beckham pulled out of me and flipped me over. I was so startled by the sudden movement, but all I could do was let him take control.

He pushed my thighs open, popped my ass up so I was braced on my knees, my upper body flat with the mattress. I couldn't help but feel exposed in the best of ways. He covered my back with his chest. It was only a second before I felt him reach between us and place his dick right back in my pussy. I instantly started to feel my lust rise to the surface as another orgasm rushed to the surface with this new position.

"That's it," he whispered, groaning. "You're so hot and wet, and so slick for me." He started pushing in and pulling out of me faster, harder.

The scent of sex and sweat filled the room. The sounds of our heavy breathing surrounded us. The passion between us was intense, so tangible I felt it cover my skin in the most delicious sensations.

I realized I heard him fucking me, the sound of his cock moving in and out of me, the wet suctioning erotic and obscene. The sensations consumed every part of me. It was this stimulating, auditory pleasure-filled sensation.

I was on my belly for only a few moments longer, and then I was suddenly being flipped onto my back, Beckham's massive body over me. I loved the way he was taking control, moving me around the way he wanted.

It was hard not to watched the play of his muscles bunch and flex under Beckham's skin as he moved. It was like watching a predator being stealthy, deliberate. And as I found myself lifting my hands and touching his chest, there was nothing but desire moving through me. His groan from my touch fueled me on.

"Lenora," he murmured and closed his eyes as I continue to run my hands over his body. "I need you to get off again for me. I need that."

Oh, I had no doubt I'd give him what he wanted.

Closing my eyes and breathing out harshly, I wanted him to know where I was right now. "Beckham," I gasped. "I'm going to come again." And I was, so hard I knew it would be just as powerful as the first one that claimed me.

"*Fuck*. Give it to me."

I gasped as soon as that last word left his lips.

"Milk me, baby."

And just like that, I did.

My pussy muscles clenched around his girth,

and he grunted in response, his hips slamming hard against mine as if he couldn't stop himself form doing the action.

He closed his eyes and growled erotically, and he clenched his jaw tightly. "Here I come."

I forced myself to keep my eyes open. I wanted to see him get off because of *me*.

"Fuck, Lenora," he hissed. "I love you so much." He thrust in deep and stilled. He did this again and again, over and over until I was panting.

Feeling his body on top of me, his thick cock *in* me, had me orgasming again unexpectedly. That pleasure stole my sanity.

My inner muscles clamped down hard, and we both moaned, the ecstasy on his face clear. My pussy squeezed his cock again as my orgasm raged on.

"Fuck, Lenora. Yeah, baby. That's *so* it. Squeeze my dick; work for it." His filthy words were an instant accelerant in me and I gasped in reaction.

With his huge body over mine, I felt every hard muscle in him tense further as I watched Beckham find his own orgasm. It was incredible to see him finally losing control. He groaned harshly again, bucking against me, emptying himself into my body. And I greedily accepted it all.

"Beckham," I whispered. He was buried deep in

me, filling me, making me his. I felt his big body shaking as he let go. His cum filled me up, making me take every last drop.

After long seconds, Beckham finally relaxed atop me, his big, muscular form making me feel so small and feminine.

Our bodies were damp from sweat, our breathing starting to calm. All I wanted to do was stay like this, to just be in our own bubble where nothing would touch us.

Beckham rolled off me but kept me right up against him and whispered, "I love you so much, Lenora. I really do."

I closed my eyes, nothing else mattering except this moment, except what we'd shared and what was to come.

"I could stay like this forever."

I hummed in agreement. "Then let's do just that."

He chuckled softly and tightened his hold on me. "I'll never get enough," he whispered at the crown of my head.

I pulled back and looked up at him. He was already staring at me. The smile he gave me had everything feeling like it was perfectly aligned, like everything we'd been through, or would go through, would be worth it all.

It has *been worth it all.*

Beckham shifted on the bed and cupped the side of my face. He stared at me for long seconds before pulling me in close. I couldn't deny I loved everything about him.

"God, I love you so fucking much."

My heart totally stalled at his words.

"To have you in my life as a friend after everything would have been my dream, but now, knowing you love me the same way I love you..." He closed his eyes and shook his head slightly. "That's all I've ever wanted." He crushed me to him, and I loved it. I loved the feeling of being breathless. I loved the way his big body wrapped around mine.

"Just tell me you'll always be mine, Lenora."

I tipped my head back and looked at him. "As long as you'll always be mine."

He groaned and leaned in to kiss me. "Always."

And just like that, everything was right where it should be.

CHAPTER FOURTEEN

Lenora

The next morning

THE SOUND of someone inhaling close to my ear had me slowly opening my eyes. The sun was bright, shining right through the open window, and I groaned softly, my body pleasantly sore in all the right places. This heavy weight pressed against my back, and I closed my eyes and smiled.

Beckham.

I shifted, but Beckham groaned and held me tighter.

"It's too early for you to be getting up." His voice was deep and right by my ear. I shivered at how good it felt.

I looked over my shoulder to stare at him. His short dark hair was mussed around his head, his eyes were closed, and his naked chest was on full display. God, he was gorgeous. I lowered my gaze and looked at the sheet that was bunched around his waist, the very clear indentation of his semi-hard erection on display. I was turned on instantly. I felt the chilled air on my skin then and looked down at my chest, realizing the blanket was pooled around my waist, same as him. My breasts were on full display, my nipples hardening. As if Beckham sensed that, he slid his hand up and cupped a mound, sliding his palm against the peaks and pulling a moan from me.

God.

"You feel incredible," he whispered against my shoulder, and I shifted, my ass rubbing against his stiff dick.

I wanted him to take me again, but I needed to go to the bathroom and definitely freshen up.

I reached for the sheet, but he stopped me, chuckling. "Don't hide yourself from me, Lenora. You're too fucking pretty for that."

My body felt flushed instantly.

"Well, pretty or not, this girl has to go to the

bathroom." He chuckled and let go of me, and I looked over my shoulder to stare at him.

He rolled onto his back and placed an arm over his face, but I could still see he watched me, his eyes hooded, his expression sexy. I took in the sight of his six-pack, of his defined pecs and bulging biceps, and I wanted to lean down and lick every inch of him.

Beckham owned me last night. There was no other way to put it. I was sore between my thighs, and I knew it wasn't just because he was massive in every sense, but also because I'd given him my virginity.

My heart fluttered at the very thought that he'd given me every part of himself too, that not only did he claim my innocence, but I had his forever as well. A pleasant discomfort and twinge of pain when I moved said he'd certainly made last night memorable. And as I felt the stickiness between my legs, the product of how I'd made him go over the edge, his cum on my inner thighs, I felt this sense of excitement and arousal thrum through my veins.

"I'll be back," I said and watched the slow grin spread across his lips.

"I'll be waiting, baby."

My heart jumped in my throat at his endearment.

Although I was very much aware of my nudity, and a little uncomfortable with flaunting it in this morning light in front of Beckham, when I looked over my shoulder and saw the way his gaze was trained on my ass then saw the massive erection he sported, this powerful feeling came over me.

The small bathroom attached to his room was convenient, and once inside, I shut the door and stared at myself in the mirror.

The bathroom was tiny, with a single-person shower stall and an array of manly looking things on the counter. Everything in here smelled like Beckham. Memories of what we'd done last night, of how our skin had been sweaty and pressed together, played through my mind. As I stared at my naked body in the mirror, I noticed there were small bruises on my hips, and when I looked down, I saw there were fingerprint-sized blue and purple marks on my thighs as well. Heat bloomed in me, and I instantly got wet between my legs.

Beckham had given me these, a mark. His mark.

After using the bathroom, gargling some mouthwash, and running my fingers through my "the morning after a good fuck" hair, I headed back into the bedroom and saw Beckham lying in the same place, his arm still over his eyes. But when he heard me enter, he pushed himself up and grinned. God, I loved him so much. His muscles flexed and bunched with the littlest shift of his body, and I felt myself heat all over again.

When I was close enough to the bed, Beckham pulled me down onto the mattress, and I happily laid beside him, curling against his big, muscular body, resting my head on his chest, and listening to the beat of his heart.

For long moments, we just lay there, needing nowhere to go, no rush, just letting the aftereffects of finally being truthful to each other, finally giving ourselves over, consume every part of us.

"How is your dad?" I finally asked. I expected him to tense, to pull away. This was absolutely a sensitive subject, painful. But he never stopped running his fingers up and down my arm, and he kept me close, stayed relaxed.

"He's really well, actually. He asks about you all the time."

I felt a twinge of guilt that I hadn't stayed in contact with Rob as much as I should have. He'd been a part of my life for years. But after everything, I'd felt weird, guilty. I felt if he saw me, he'd only be reminded of my mother and what she did.

"I miss him. I need to be better at checking in with him."

Beckham kissed the top of my head. "He'd really love that." We stayed silent for a few seconds. "He met someone, by the way."

I felt a smile filter across my face at the sound of that. I sat up slightly and looked down at his face, saw the smile he wore as well.

"He really likes her."

I felt happiness for Rob and was so thankful my mother hadn't ruined his life. "I'm glad. I'm really glad he's happy again."

Beckham pulled me back down against him, and I wrapped my arm around his waist. I was thankful he didn't talk about my mother, didn't ask about her again. She didn't need to intrude on this moment. I'd come to terms long ago that the life she led didn't include me. And when it did, it was only on her terms. And that's not a life I wanted to have.

I didn't want to be someone's backup, someone to stroke their ego, to make them feel better.

I wanted to be someone's priority, and I found that with Beckham.

"I hope this goes without saying, but I don't want you to leave, Lenora. I want you to stay here with me, to share this room with me... to be mine."

God, I'd wanted to hear him say that for so long.

"There is no arrangement. There never was. As soon as you asked to move in with me, I knew I'd make things right and make you stay here with me anyway I could. There was no way I could have let you go again."

I shifted on the mattress so I could look at him. I wanted to stare in his eyes as I listened.

"I'm not saying I'm perfect. I'm far from it. I'll probably make mistakes down the road, piss you off, make you wish you could punch me in the face."

I couldn't help but smile.

His expression sobered. "But know this. I love you, Lenora, more than I've ever loved anyone or anything in this fucking world. And that'll never change. It'll only grow as time passes. I'm in this for the long haul with you. Forever." He cupped my cheek and leaned in to kiss me softly. "And I think you want that too."

The way he said it was poised a little like a question, and so to reassure him, I kissed him back. "That's all I've wanted for so long," I murmured against his mouth.

"I want you as my wife someday, Lenora. Someday soon. So fucking soon. I want to have a family with you, make a home with you. I want the world with you." Beckham pulled me in for a hug, and I melted against him.

I'd finally gotten that happily ever after I sure as hell deserved. And God, it felt good.

EPILOGUE ONE

Beckham
Six months later

I STARED at Lenora and tried to wrap my head around what she just told me. It was like someone just kicked me in the balls.

For the last year, she'd been living with me. We'd made this house a home for both of us. She decorated it, helped renovate the upstairs. She even had her own little room, one where she could read in the nook I created for her by the window, where she had her many books lined up in the bookcases I'd gotten for her at her favorite antique shop.

And I'd never been happier.

And although I always dreamed about this moment, I hadn't thought it would be yet.

"Please say something," she said so softly I almost didn't hear her. She kept twisting her hands together, her nervousness tangible.

I didn't want to make her feel this way.

Lenora was having my baby. She was pregnant, carrying my child, and I was going to be a father.

"I—I—" Hell, I had no fucking idea what to say. The sonogram picture she'd given me to break the news was still in my hand, and I stared at that black-and-white picture. That was my baby, although it didn't look much aside from a little bean-shaped thing. But it was my baby. "I don't know what to say, baby." I was being honest.

"I took three pregnancy tests when I realized how late I was. So I made an appointment with the doctor. I didn't know they were going to do the ultrasound." She was still twisting her hands together. "I should have just talked to you about it, but... here we are."

I looked at her again, anticipation and excitement filling me even though on the outside I probably looked shell-shocked. I couldn't help it. She watched me with wide eyes, her lips parted, her fear tangible. She was afraid of my reaction. Could she possibly think I wouldn't want this?

"Please say something, Beckham." She took a stuttering breath. "Are you just as scared as I am? I know this isn't planned—"

"Lenora, baby, you're pregnant." I grinned from ear-to-ear. I pulled her in for an embrace and buried my face in her hair, inhaling deeply. God, the woman I loved was pregnant with my child.

"I wasn't sure if showing you the picture was a good thing, but when I saw the ultrasound from when I got the pregnancy confirmed, I thought— hoped—you would want to see it."

I pulled back and cupped her cheeks, kissing her until we were both breathless. "This is all I've ever wanted. A family with you, Lenora." Yeah, we were young, but we were also doing well in life, and I had a good job. I could provide for her and our children.

"I don't want you working at the café anymore." I realized what I said. "I mean, you can if you want, you know, being an independent female and all, but I want to take care of you." I chuckled softly when she smiled. "At least after the baby is born, think about staying home for a while? Let me take care of you two."

I saw the amusement in her eyes. Yeah, I'd been

possessive before, but knowing she was carrying my child made me downright territorial and protective.

"You're happy? This doesn't freak you out?"

I shook my head right way. "No fucking way." I leaned in and kissed her softly, so softly.

"I'm a little scared, Beckham."

I couldn't blame her. This was all new. But it would be good, perfect. "Let me show you, prove to you that I won't fuck this up, Lenora. Let me show you I'll be the best man, the best father to our baby, and the best future husband to you that I can be."

She smiled, cupped my cheek with one hand, and said in a soft voice, "You're already the best partner I could ask for. I know you'll be the very best father too."

I pulled her in close and just held her. I'd never been happier than when I was with Lenora, and right now, the euphoria that filled me told me so much. It told me that she was my soulmate, that I was exactly where I was supposed to be.

I was with exactly who I was supposed to be with.

EPILOGUE TWO

Beckham
One year later

I'D NEVER FUCKING GET tired of this, never wish I'd done things differently. Because no matter what, no matter how things had progressed, transgressed... no matter how life had changed so drastically, I knew I was the luckiest bastard in the world.

I had my woman, the girl I loved for longer than I even wanted to admit.

The mother of my child.

My wife.

And as I took my woman, claimed her, made her mine over and over again, my pleasure increased tenfold like it always did.

I stared at my woman's breasts as they bounced up and down as she rode the hell out of my cock. God, she was so perfect. I was trying so damn hard not to get off right now. Her inner muscles clenched rhythmically around my dick, and I had to grit my teeth so I didn't come right then and there. I wanted her to get off, wanted to see the expression of euphoria cover her face just once more before I gave in to my own pleasure.

She was my priority, not just in the bedroom but in life.

Her and my children. Always.

Wrapping my arm around her waist and grabbing onto her ass cheek with my other hand, I rose up just enough that I could shift and have her back to the mattress. I slid all the way back into her and groaned, my eyes closing on their own as ecstasy claimed me. She was so fucking hot and tight.

I leaned back on my haunches and looked down at where our bodies were connected.

"Fuck, baby." Those words left me on a strangled groan as I saw the way her pussy stretched around my cock. She was all pink and soaked flesh and stretched so wide around the girth of my cock that it actually felt like I got harder inside her. Lenora's eyes widened, and I knew she was close to getting off again.

I placed my thumb right on her clit, rubbed the hell out of that little bud, and couldn't take my gaze off of her cunt. Lenora cried out and arched her back, thrust her breasts out, and closed her eyes. I finally let myself go as I watched her come undone.

I leaned forward, bracing my hands on the bed beside her head, and grunted as I came right along with her.

Without thinking, because all I wanted to do was kiss her, I captured her lips with mine. I filled her up, knew when I pulled out of her tight body all my cum would slip from her and soak the sheets beneath her perfect ass.

With my cock softening inside her and our tongues pressing back and forth against each other, I let a contented sigh leave me. I forced myself to lean back an inch. "Lenora. God, baby, you never cease to amaze me." I leaned down and kissed her once more before pulling out of her with a grunt of disappointment. I rolled to my side and took her with me. She was soft where I was hard. I fucking loved her curves, loved that she had even more now after having our baby.

I leaned down and kissed her on the crown of

her head. "You make me deliriously happy." She cuddled in closer to me, and I'd never get tired of that feeling.

The sound of the baby crying came through the monitor, and with one more kiss to her head, I stood. I covered her with a blanket and looked down at her. My wife looked good and fucked. "Let me go get him."

I put on a pair of sweats and headed into Sylas's bedroom. I saw our son squirming on the mattress, his little arms outstretched. I knew there was a massive scream about to be let out, so I cradled Sylas to my chest, rubbed his tiny back, and my son gave a mighty cry of hunger. There it was. "You want Momma?" I headed back into our room and saw Lenora already sitting up, her glorious breasts on display as she knew what time it was.

She held her hands out for the baby, and I gave her our son, watching as she cradled him so gently. I sat on the edge of the bed and for the next twenty minutes watched the mother of my child feed our baby. It was beautiful. Sylas was already back to sleep, and I could see Lenora had no plans on moving him as he slept against her chest.

She looked at me with such love and devotion in her eyes it actually had my heart skipping a beat.

"I love you, Beckham," she said softly.

"I love you, baby. God, I love you so much and the life we've created." I leaned in close and placed my nose at her temple, inhaling deeply. I smelled the shampoo she used in her hair and caught the faint scent of baby lotion that she applied to Sylas after his bath. I couldn't help but smile.

This was my world. She'd been my world even before I knew it.

And I'd never take that for granted.

JENIKA SNOW

MOUNTAIN MAN (A REAL MAN)

By Jenika Snow

www.JenikaSnow.com

Jenika_Snow@Yahoo.com

Copyright © March 2020 by Jenika Snow

First ebook edition © March 2020 by Jenika Snow

Cover design by: Lori Jackson Design

Content Editor: Kayla Robichaux

MOUNTAIN

There's nothing tame about him.

MAN

I was known in town as old money but lived off the land, a present-day caveman. They called me the town recluse, dubbed me a mountain man, antisocial. It was true.

But then she came into my life and turned everything I knew upside down.

It started with Bailey getting lost in the woods and finding herself on my doorstep.

She was sweet and innocent, half my age, and I had no control when the arousal built between us that night.

It ended with me taking her virginity in a passion-filled night.

But then she was gone, and I should have gone after her, thrown her over my shoulder, and demanded she was mine.

Four years later and our paths cross again. I thought I was stronger, able to control myself, but where Bailey was concerned, there was no doubt she called the shots. She owned my heart.

She'd gotten under my skin in the best of ways, and I knew this time around, I wouldn't let her get away.

CHAPTER ONE

Bailey

I KNEW COMING BACK to Mountain Falls meant I'd run into him.

The man I'd lost my virginity to four years ago—on my eighteenth birthday.

Gavin Taylor was a recluse, someone who stayed away from others, because he was that antisocial. He'd built a cabin a shitload of miles from town, high in the mountains; the only company he had was the wilderness that surrounded him.

He was a mountain man in every sense of the word—gruff, rough around the edges, take-no-shit from anyone, and an overall caveman demeanor.

Four years later and here I was, back in my

hometown because of a job opportunity. I'd jumped at the chance to come back when I was offered a position in the pharmacy. A part of me missed "home," missed family and friends. But it was the bigger part of me, the carnal part, that wanted to return, because of *him*. Gavin.

I'd never stopped thinking about him or that night when I wondered off the trail during a hike and came to his cabin.

I'd been cold and tired, thirsty and hungry. I'd gotten lost, found myself at his front door. He'd let me in, fed me, gave me something warm to drink, and let me sit by the fire. Aside from first name introductions, he hadn't said one word the whole time, but as the hours passed, as I realized I didn't want to leave, that there was this pull I had toward him, things... changed.

Then I asked him for something warmer to drink, a glass of that whiskey he had sitting on the coffee table in front of him. I'd blurted out I was twenty-one, a lie and three years older than what I actually was. And he'd given me some without even saying a word, without questioning me.

He'd poured me the whiskey, handed me the glass, and after I finished it, I started feeling a buzz. It was the first time I ever drank, and I was pretty proud of myself for not throwing up. But it wasn't just the alcohol that had me warming. It was the intense attraction, arousal I felt for Gavin.

That's when I knew things would move to the next level.

And then I'd been honest, told him I was only eighteen. He said we shouldn't do this; it was wrong.

I told him nothing had ever felt more right.

And on that night, he'd taken my virginity with so much passion and rawness that I'd never been with a man since.

Because Gavin had ruined all other guys for me.

And as they say, the rest was history.

Although it's not history, because all I thought about in these past four years was him between my legs, the way he made me feel... the way he made me come.

I pulled myself back to the present, put the last bag of groceries in my car, and shut the trunk, standing there and looking around. A part of me thought I'd see Gavin as soon as I came into Mountain Falls.

A part of me had hoped.

But I knew better. He didn't like people. And I couldn't blame him. The town of Mountain Falls, despite how beautiful and picturesque it was, was one of those towns where everyone knew everything and everyone's business.

No secret was safe in this town. Although, as far as I knew, that night I lost my virginity to Gavin would forever stay between us. Because I sure as hell knew if anyone in this town heard about it, they would let me know.

I got into my car and smoothed my hands down my jeans. I don't know why I was so nervous. I didn't even know if he still lived in Mountain Falls. But in my heart, in my gut, I was sure he did.

Aside from the few things I'd learned about him after our encounter, I realized Gavin was just as much of a mystery to me as he was to everyone else. He was a fourth-generation Mountain Falls resident, his great grandfather striking it rich with oil, which was technically passed down. Gavin, being the only living Taylor now and having no heir, owned all of it. He was wealthy beyond belief, but he didn't live outside of his means. In fact, he owned nothing lavish, as far as I remembered.

God, what was it about him that had me so consumed all these years? I could've blamed it on the fact that he'd been my first, but I knew that wasn't the case. He was the strong, silent type, and I had a feeling he didn't let people in to know who the real Gavin was.

He was very much the tall, dark, and handsome type who had a mysteriousness to him that intrigued the hell out of me.

Had he thought about me all these years? Did he wonder what I'd been doing, if I'd met anyone, if I'd been with anyone?

God, the very thought of him with another woman had my stomach clenching and distaste taking hold. I meant it when I said he ruined all other men for me. Everyone else seemed like... boys.

I tried to push thoughts of Gavin aside and focus on the present. But that had never been easy. I headed to my parents' house, a temporary situation until the legalities of renting the duplex were squared up and the owner and I could finalize everything.

And as I drove, the only thing that kept playing through my mind was how I wanted to get lost in those woods again and find myself on Gavin's doorstep.

CHAPTER TWO

Gavin

I PULLED my pick-up to a stop in front of my cabin, cut the engine, and glanced over at the porch. Bear, my Tibetan Mastiff, was sprawled out on the wood. He lifted his big head, saw it was me, and promptly went back to sleep. He'd been one hell of a guard dog back in the day, but now that the vet considered him geriatric, he'd been retired and was living out the rest of his days sunbathing instead of protecting the property. And that was fine by me.

He earned this downtime.

I climbed out of the vehicle and shut the door, walking around the side and looking in the back of the truck. The bed was filled with lumber, my ax situated between the logs, the handle worn and damaged from years of use.

All morning, I'd been out on the property cutting down dead trees, stockpiling the wood for winter later this year. There were things that always had to be done around the cabin or the property, the hundred acres that surrounded my home having been in my family for generations. The cabin had once been my father's, one he and my grandfather had built together before Dad married my mother and I was born.

And after my parents passed away in a tragic accident while overseas for their anniversary over a decade ago, I renovated it in their honor.

In their memory.

I added on to it, even though it was just me living there. I didn't need the extra space, but it had given me something to do, and I knew my mother had always wanted more space. I did it for her.

It also kept me busy. It didn't matter if I had money in the bank, more than I'd ever need in a lifetime. I lived off the land as much as I could, did repairs myself, and didn't spend money on anything that I didn't absolutely have to. Hell, my pick-up truck was twenty years old, rusted around the wheels, with a cassette player that didn't even work in the dash. But it was a beast on these uneven mountain roads, and it got the job done when need be.

I grabbed my ax and headed toward the porch, setting it by the front door and then turning to look at Bear. He made a gruff sound when I leaned down and scratched behind his ear but otherwise stayed lying down, obviously wanting to get back to sleep.

I went into the cabin, and like always for the last four years, my focus was trained right in front of that fireplace. All these years later, and I could still remember the way she smelled, the way she felt pressed against me, and the warmth of her body licking over my naked skin as I thrust inside her.

I shouldn't have done any of that. She'd been far too young, only eighteen. It was wrong, being twice her age and having just met her, but she'd been the first person that made me feel... something.

Bailey made me feel something more than this void.

And I let the whiskey start doing the talking, let my body and arousal control the situation. And I had absolutely no strength where she was concerned, none when she touched my arm and leaned in close, telling me she felt something between us that she wanted to explore. And when she admitted to me that she was lonely, that she just wanted to feel alive, all self-control I had completely fucking snapped.

Because I felt the same way.

I lifted my hand and rubbed the back of my head. Fuck, I was getting turned on. She'd been the first woman I'd slept with in years. She'd been the only woman I'd been with since. And I wanted her again and again, over and over until neither of us could walk.

I only wanted her, only wanted to feel how soft she was again, how good she felt as I thrust inside her. She'd been so tight and wet, so fucking hot.

Fuck, I was obsessed with her. There was no other explanation for the fact that I couldn't keep my mind off her, and even all these years later, she was still the first thing I thought about when I woke up, and the last thing on my mind as I jerked myself off before bed.

I growled low and tossed my keys on the table. I had a bad fucking case of blue balls. Had them for four fucking years. But no other woman would compare to her. No other woman could have me feeling an iota of the kinds of things Baylee had.

I braced my hands on the counter and breathed out slowly, closing my eyes. That was a bad fucking idea, because the image of her popped into my head, one of her laid out in front of my fireplace, her dark hair fanned out over the rug, her lips parted, and her eyes wide as I thrust all my hard inches into her virgin pussy.

My dick was stiff, a fucking lead pipe hanging between my legs. I reached down and palmed myself behind my jeans, and all that did was have my balls draw up even tighter to my body and the need to go jerk one off in a cold shower riding me hard.

But no. I wasn't going to give in to my carnal desires. Not until it was time for me to lie in bed and stare at the fucking ceiling as I pictured filling her up with my seed.

After I claimed her in my cabin all those years ago, I searched her out, knowing I wouldn't be able to stop needing her, knowing I wanted her by my side. She was the first person, the first woman, who had a hold of my heart, who refused to let it go even after she left. And I knew no other woman would hold a flame to her. Ever.

But she'd left town, gone to college. I overheard those little details at the grocery store when I was picking up a month's worth of food. And I nearly cursed right then and there, stormed off like a fucking caveman, because I couldn't get what I wanted. And that was Bailey.

I kept myself busy with work around the cabin and the property, even more so once I knew I couldn't have her. I'd been pissed at myself for not making her see we were meant for each other. I was fucking angry I'd let her get away.

At this point, it was all busywork, but it was manual labor that would not only tire me out but hopefully keep my mind preoccupied. That was until I thought about her again, which seemed to be every other fucking minute.

Fuck, I either needed professional help or I just needed to find out where she was and go to her, demand she was mine like I was a barbarian. And that actually seemed very fucking realistic.

ABOUT THE AUTHOR

Want to read more by Jenika Snow? Find all her titles here:

http://jenikasnow.com/bookshelf/

Find the author at:

www.JenikaSnow.com

Jenika_Snow@yahoo.com

Printed in Great Britain
by Amazon